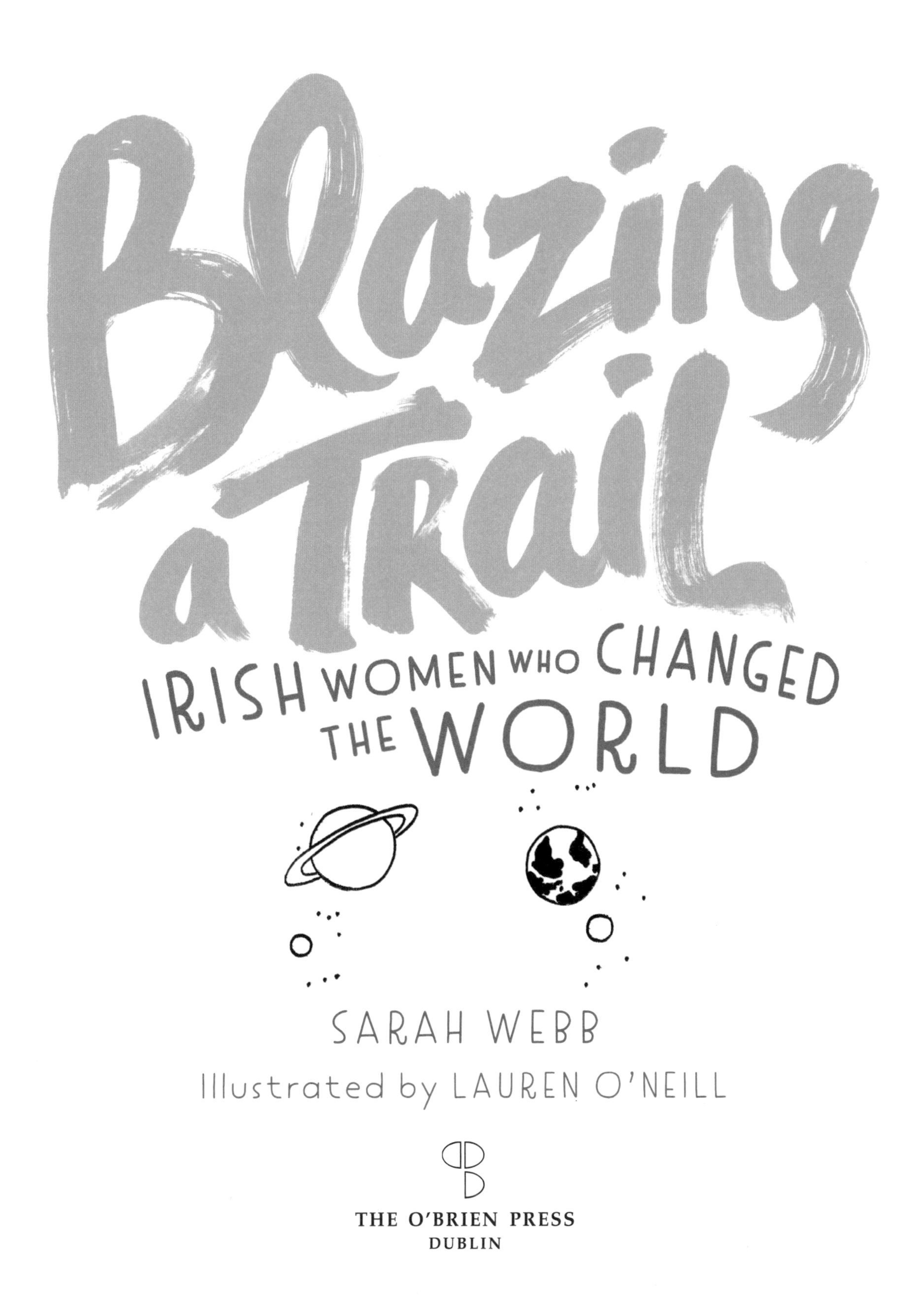

Blazing a Trail

Irish Women Who Changed the World

Sarah Webb

Illustrated by Lauren O'Neill

THE O'BRIEN PRESS
DUBLIN

First published 2018 by
The O'Brien Press Ltd.
12 Terenure Road East,
Rathgar, Dublin 6, D06 HD27,
Ireland.
Tel: +353 1 4923333; Fax: +353 1 4922777
E-mail: books@obrien.ie; Website: www.obrien.ie
The O'Brien Press is a member of Publishing Ireland.
Reprinted 2018.

ISBN: 978-1-78849-004-7

10 9 8 7 6 5 4 3 2
23 22 21 20 19 18

Printed by EDELVIVES, Spain.
The paper in this book is produced using pulp from managed forests.

Sarah Webb was the dlr Writer in Residence 2016–2017.
She worked on this book during her residency.

Dedications –
This one's for my mother, Melissa Webb, who first showed me how to be brave; my sisters, Kate and Emma, two wonderfully courageous women; and my daughter, Amy-Rose, who has inherited the brave gene in spades! (SW)
Dedicated to the memory of Phyllis Wilde, one of my all-time favourite ladies. (LO'N)

Acknowledgements –
With thanks to everyone at The O'Brien Press for their hard work and support, especially my editor Aoife K. Walsh, designer Emma Byrne and Lauren O'Neill for her stunning illustrations. This book was truly a team effort! I'd also like to thank Nigel Curtin and Marian Keyes from dlr Libraries, Caroline Carswell, Maria Delaney, Martina Devlin, Professor Peter Gallagher, Mary Hannigan, Lindie Naughton, Tony O'Brien, Marion Palmer and Margaret Ward for all their help with the research. Thanks to Mary Moran for the Máire Ní Chinnéide quote from her book, *A Game of Our Own: Camogie's Story*. (SW)
A huge thank you to Sarah Webb for writing this wonderful book, and to the whole team at The O'Brien Press who made it a reality. Special thanks to editor Aoife K. Walsh and designer Emma Byrne who really made everything come together. (LO'N)

Published in:

CONTENTS

About this Book

SARAH WEBB SAYS:

At school I was taught that men were the history makers, the doctors, the artists, the scientists. Later, when I was older, I discovered that this simply was not true. There have always been remarkable women shaping our world, and in this book I wanted to shine a light on some of the amazing female Irish pioneers. In selecting the women, I had two main criteria: they had to be remarkable in their field, and they had to encourage and support other women along the way.

These women didn't have to be good, they had to be outstanding. Even better than the men, they had to be braver, fight harder, study longer. They also had to put up with people telling them that women weren't strong enough to be aviators or clever enough to be scientists or even to vote!

I have adored travelling with some of Ireland's most inspiring women, and their courage and tenacity will remain with me for many years to come. I hope every person who reads this book, young or old, will find someone who inspires them and helps them blaze their own trail into the future.

LAUREN O'NEILL SAYS:

When I was a child the two things I loved most were reading and drawing, and for me they went hand in hand. I imagined princesses and heroines who did extraordinary things, and I would draw these characters again and again. It was my way of reliving their adventures after their stories were over.

Now, it is books like *Blazing a Trail* that make me realise something exciting: Irish history is full of real-life inspirational women who have shaped the country and world we live in. These illustrations are my tribute to just a few of them and they are my own interpretation of their everyday lives, their passions, personalities and achievements. I hope they'll give young readers a sense of what it means to be a trailblazer, and inspire them to change the world in their own unique way.

'Terra marique potens O'Maille'
(O'Malley, strong on land and sea.), written on
Granuaile's tomb

Granuaile

CLAN LEADER AND SEA CAPTAIN

c.1530 – c.1603

The sea was in Granuaile's blood. Her father, a powerful Mayo chieftain, owned one of the largest fleets of boats in Ireland.

From a young age Granuaile (also called Grace O'Malley or Gráinne Ní Mháille) was determined to go to sea, but her father would not allow it. 'You're a girl,' he said, 'your hair will get caught in the rigging.' So Granuaile cut all her hair off! She was soon leading expeditions to Spain and Portugal to trade wool and cattle hides for salt and cloth. She became known as a fearless and gifted sailor and navigator.

Granuaile married Donal O'Flaherty when she was sixteen, and they had three children. She commanded her husband's fleet, stopping ships coming into Galway harbour and demanding a toll. If a captain refused, she took some of the ship's goods. She became known as the Pirate Queen of Connacht.

When Donal was murdered, Granuaile moved to Clare Island with two hundred followers. In 1566 she married Richard An Iarainn Burke and they had one son, Tibbot. The English governor of Connacht did not like Granuaile's wild and 'unwomanly' behaviour one bit. He put Tibbot in prison and tried to take away her ships and land. But Granuaile wasn't having this. She sailed to London to meet Queen Elizabeth I in Greenwich Castle. Speaking in Latin, she asked the queen to give back the stolen land and to release her son. Elizabeth was so impressed with Granuaile that she granted her wishes.

Granuaile is said to be buried on Clare Island, in the medieval abbey overlooking her beloved sea.

In Granuaile's time, Ireland was covered by huge forests with wild boar, deer and wolves. With very few roads or bridges, it could take a month to get from Dublin to Galway.

When Queen Elizabeth I had a new map of Ireland made, she asked that Granuaile's name be included as a Mayo chieftain.

Ireland's old Brehon Laws allowed women to fight in battles, divorce their husbands and keep their own property after they married.

Maria Edgeworth

BESTSELLING AUTHOR AND EDUCATIONIST

1768–1849

Maria was the second of twenty-two brothers and sisters and lived most of her life at her family's home at Edgeworthstown in County Longford, after being born and educated in England. She was an extremely bright and able girl and by the age of fifteen was doing all the household accounts. She also wrote stories to entertain her siblings, like 'Simple Susan' and 'Lazy Lawrence', tales that taught them to be good.

When she was twenty-eight, she published her first book, *Letters for Literary Ladies*, which encouraged education for girls, a very unusual idea at the time. Another book, *Practical Education*, which she wrote with her writer and inventor father Richard, talked about the importance of playtime for children, and became popular in America.

When her father died, Maria bought the family house from her brother with the money from her books. She ran the house herself, although she kindly pretended that her brother was in charge. During the Irish Famine she wrote a book called *Orlandino* to raise money for food and she made sure her tenants had enough to eat (as long as they had paid their rent).

She was one of the most famous writers of her day and is now best known for her novel *Castle Rackrent*, about a wealthy Irish family, told by one of their servants. It was published in 1800 and became a huge success. It is said to have started a new type of book: the Anglo-Irish Big House novel. Maria's children's books are an important part of the library collection of Trinity College, Dublin.

Castle Rackrent is still in print today. It is read by students of literature all over the world.

Jane Austen loved Maria's writing and Sir Walter Scott called her 'the Great Maria'. Other writers, like William Wordsworth and Lord Byron, travelled a long way to visit her.

Irish writers who have followed in Maria's footsteps include: Somerville and Ross, Elizabeth Bowen, Maeve Binchy, Maeve Brennan, Molly Keane, Mary Lavin, Kate O'Brien, and children's writers Eilís Dillon and Patricia Lynch.

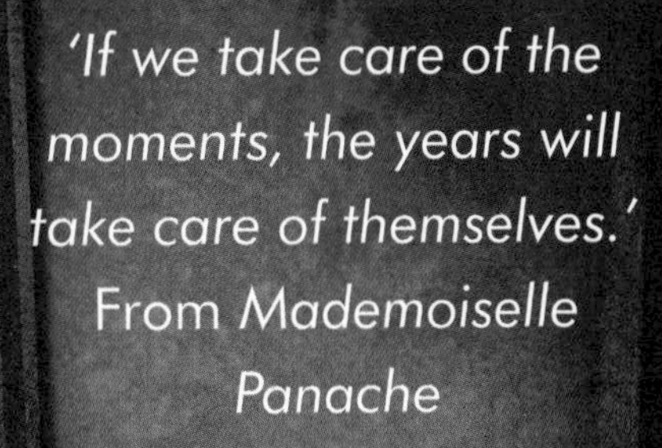
'If we take care of the moments, the years will take care of themselves.'
From Mademoiselle Panache

'Was I not a girl, I would be a soldier!'
Dr James Barry

Dr James Barry

DARING SURGEON

c.1799–1865

Margaret Bulkley was one of the first women in the world to study medicine and become a doctor, more than fifty years before women were allowed in college.

Born in Cork, Margaret was the niece of the Irish painter James Barry. When her father was put in prison for not paying his bills, Margaret and her mother and sister moved to London. There she met her uncle's friends, including General Francisco de Miranda, who was a revolutionary from Venezuela.

A clever and determined girl, Margaret wanted to become a surgeon and join General Miranda's military campaign. So, using her inheritance and presenting herself as a man, she studied medicine at Edinburgh University. But by the time Margaret graduated, General Miranda was in prison, so she bravely joined the British Army taking the name 'Dr James Barry'. Margaret would live as James for the rest of her life.

James was sent to Cape Town, South Africa, where he was so good at his job he was quickly made Medical Inspector. Although known for being fiery and short-tempered, James treated his patients with respect. He was a highly skilled surgeon and a progressive thinker, and he gave free medical treatment to poor women. In 1826 he performed one of the first caesarean sections in the world where both the mother and the baby survived. The baby was named James Barry Munnik in his honour.

When James died it was discovered that he was physically a woman. This shocked the British Army. They cancelled his military funeral and stopped the newspapers from covering the story. After everything he had achieved! Finally, in the 1950s, the historian Isobel Rae found Dr James Barry's records and began to piece together his extraordinary life.

In the 1700s Dubliner Kit Cavanagh disguised herself as a man and joined the British Army to look for her husband. She found him but liked being a soldier so much she stayed!

Dr Barry's favourite drink was goat's milk and he always travelled with a goat. He was a vegetarian and loved animals.

He kept many dogs during his life, all called Psyche, and also had a pet parrot.

Anna Haslam

SUFFRAGIST

1829–1922

Anna Maria Fisher was born into a Quaker family in Youghal, County Cork. She was the second youngest of seventeen children. At the time, the Quaker religion gave more rights to their female members than other churches, and Anna was brought up believing in education and equality for everyone.

As a teenager she helped in soup kitchens during the Irish Famine, and as a young woman she helped to create cottage industries for girls, including lace-making and knitting. Anna always wanted to make Ireland a better place for women. She helped win their right to be educated, to study medicine, and to be county councillors. But her most famous fight was yet to come …

In 1876, Anna and her husband, Thomas, set up the Dublin Women's Suffrage Association, campaigning for women to win the right to vote. Anna worked as the association's secretary for thirty-seven years and never missed one meeting. Thomas suffered from bad health so, to pay the bills, Anna also ran their successful stationery shop in Rathmines.

Eventually on 14 December 1918 Irish women over thirty years of age who owned property were allowed to vote for the first time. At the polling station, Anna was cheered on and presented with a bouquet of flowers. She was ninety years old! Anna died in 1922, the same year that all women (and men) over twenty-one were given the vote.

Many men said giving women the vote would be a 'disaster for the country'!

Suffrage means the right to vote. Suffragists believed in peaceful campaigns and protests. Suffragettes believed in more direct action or 'Deeds not words'.

Other women who fought for suffrage in Ireland include Isabella Tod, authors Somerville and Ross, Countess Markievicz and Anne Jellicoe, who founded Alexandra College in 1866.

'It is not easy to keep our temper … while educated women capable … of giving a rational vote are still debarred [from voting].'

Anna Haslam

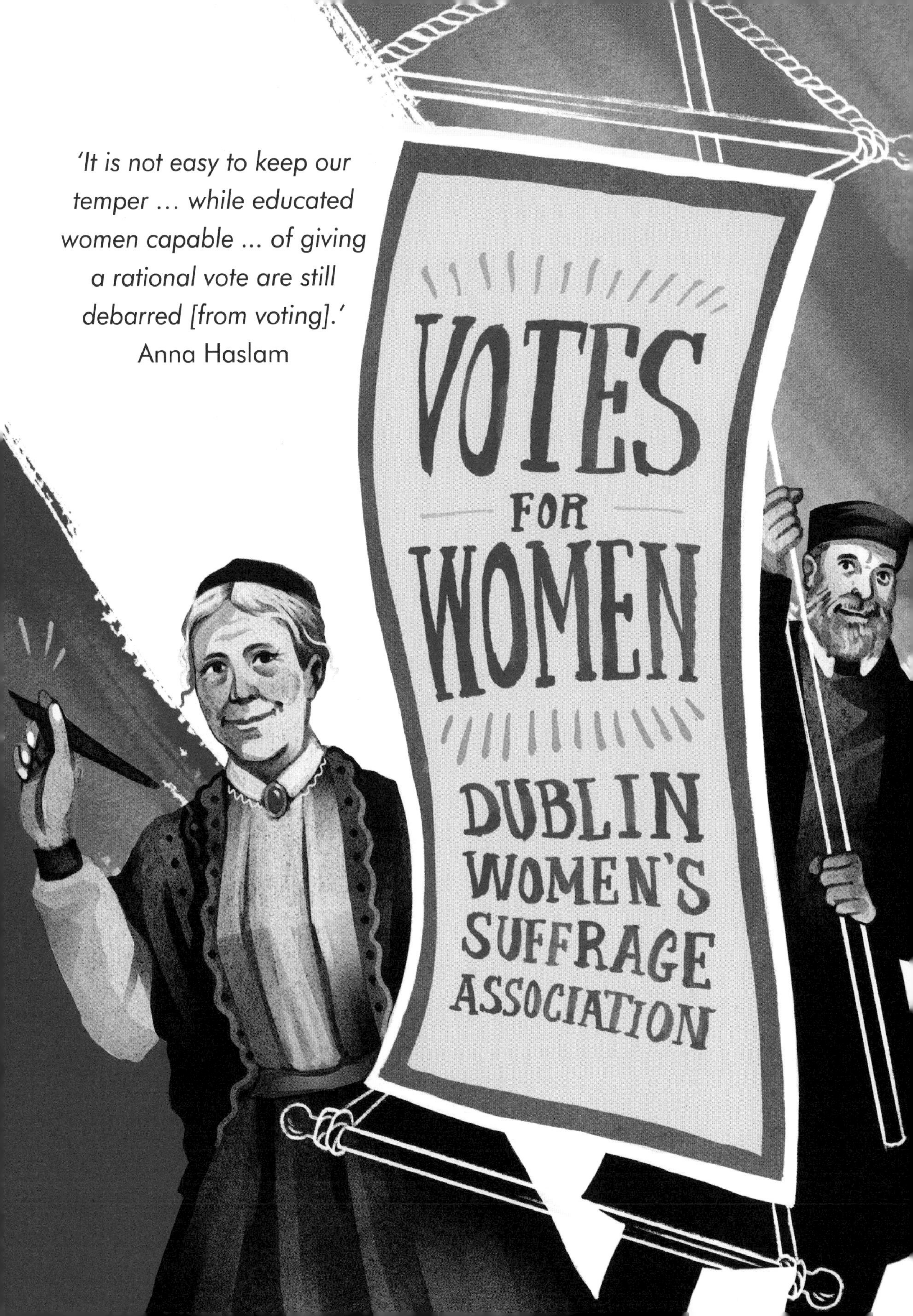

VOTES FOR WOMEN

DUBLIN WOMEN'S SUFFRAGE ASSOCIATION

Mother Jones

LABOUR ORGANISER AND CHAMPION OF CHILD WORKERS

c.1837–1930

Mary Harris was born in Cork and emigrated with her family to Canada after the Irish Famine. A few years later, she moved to America. In 1861 she married George Jones. They had four children and lived in Memphis. But sadly, they all died of yellow fever within one week. After burying her own family, Mary bravely helped other families with sick children.

Mary moved to Chicago and set up her own sewing business. Tragedy struck again, when her shop burned down in the Great Fire of Chicago. Did Mary give up? No, she did not! She looked at where workers lived, in shacks, and she looked at how rich mill owners lived, in 'tropical comfort', and she had a simple but life-changing thought: working people deserved better. And she was the woman to help them!

For the next fifty years, Mary dedicated her life to fighting for workers' rights. She became known as 'Mother Jones', the 'most dangerous woman in America', for organising strikes and campaigning for better conditions. Children as young as six were working in factories, losing fingers and arms in the machines. Mother Jones believed children should be in school, not in work. So, in 1903 she led the March of the Mill Children from Philadelphia to President Roosevelt's home on Long Island, New York. They walked over 145 kilometres, causing quite a stir and getting lots of attention. Eventually a new law was passed in most American states which increased the minimum working age to fourteen.

When she died, Mother Jones was buried in the coal miners' cemetery in Mount Olive, Illinois, surrounded by the workers she had spent her life protecting.

Mother Jones may have looked like a gentle old lady in her dark Victorian dresses and bonnets, but she fought like a lion!

She said her hatred of oppression and inequality came from her Irish roots: her rebel Irish ancestors and her early experiences of poverty as a child in Ireland.

The song 'She'll Be Coming 'round the Mountain' is said to be written about Mother Jones's travels through the mining camps in the Appalachian Mountains in America.

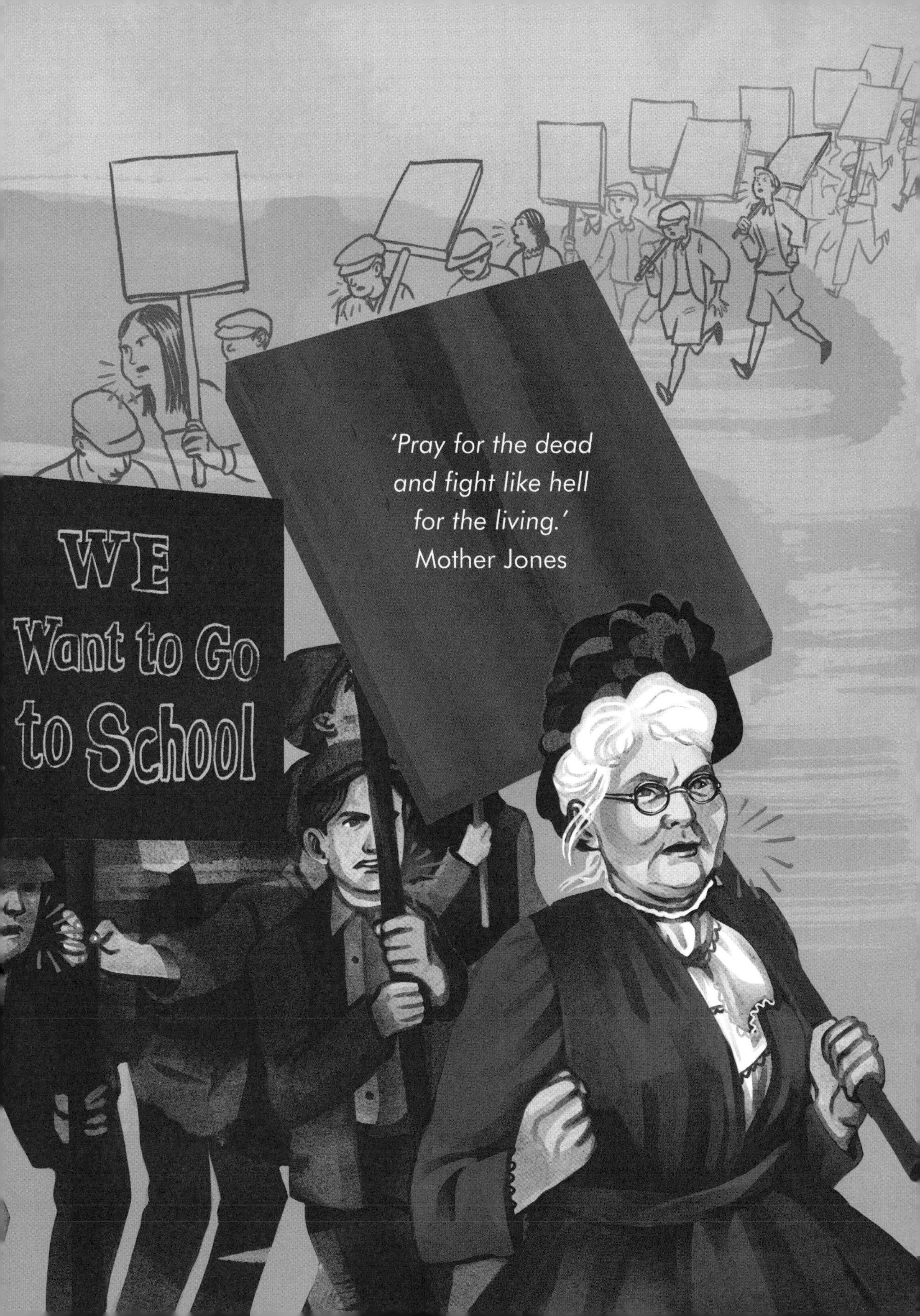

*'Pray for the dead
and fight like hell
for the living.'*
Mother Jones

'I have too much to do to be afraid.'
Nellie Cashman

Nellie Cashman

GOLD PROSPECTOR AND BUSINESSWOMAN

c.1845–1925

Ellen 'Nellie' Cashman was born near Cobh in County Cork. Her father died during the Irish Famine and she emigrated to America with her mother and sister.

Nellie was a persuasive talker and she became a brilliant businesswoman. She set up boarding houses in 'boom towns' all over America and Canada, from Tombstone in Arizona to the Klondike region of the Yukon.

In 1874 she heard that hundreds of miners were trapped in the mountains in British Columbia. So Nellie led an expedition to save them, travelling for eighty days on snow shoes and pulling supplies on a heavy sled. She nursed the men back to health and brought them all home safely, earning the name 'Angel of the Miners'.

Nellie wasn't interested in getting married, saying: 'I prefer being pals with men to being cook for one man.' She was a kind, practical woman with a very big heart. She gave money to set up hospitals for miners and their families and, when her sister died, Nellie looked after her sister's five children, paying for all of them to go to school and college.

Nellie spent the last twenty years of her life in Alaska, mining near the Arctic Circle. At age seventy-seven, she was crowned champion woman dog musher (handler) of the world when she made a seventeen-day, 1,200-kilometre trek by dog sled!

The oldest restaurant in Tombstone is called the Nellie Cashman Restaurant, and every year the city celebrates one of its most colourful heroes on Nellie Cashman Day.

Nellie was proud of her Irish roots and called one of her mines 'Parnell' after the Irish political leader Charles Stewart Parnell.

She was barely five feet tall and weighed less than forty-five kilograms, but Nellie wasn't going to let that stop her!

Sarah Purser

ARTIST, PATRON AND BUSINESSWOMAN

1848–1943

Sarah Henrietta Purser was born in Dún Laoghaire and moved to Waterford as a little girl. She was educated in Switzerland and at the Metropolitan School of Art in Dublin. Women were not allowed to study at the Royal Hibernian Academy (RHA) in Dublin, so she went to Paris to continue her art training.

When her father's businesses failed he moved to America, leaving Sarah in Dublin to earn her own money. She started painting portraits. She was honest and smart and her subjects loved talking to her, often becoming firm friends. She painted many famous Irish people including Maud Gonne and Douglas Hyde.

In 1903 Sarah founded a stained glass company, An Túr Gloine (the Tower of Glass), with Edward Martyn. Evie Hone, Wilhelmina Geddes and Harry Clarke all made glass art there. Their art has since become world-famous; thanks to Sarah's excellent sales work, it was exported to churches all over the globe.

In 1923, at the age of seventy-five, Sarah held her first solo exhibition. In the same year the RHA finally decided to open itself up to female artists, and Sarah became the first woman to hold full membership.

For many years, Sarah campaigned with the writer Lady Gregory for a modern art gallery in Dublin to host the collection of her dear friend Hugh Lane. In 1928 the Hugh Lane Gallery finally found a home in Parnell Square, where it still is today. It shows art by some of the most important Irish artists of the twentieth century: Francis Bacon, Mainie Jellett, Sean Scully along with Sarah Purser herself.

To train future art historians and art gallery curators, Sarah helped establish the history of art courses in both Trinity College, Dublin, and University College Dublin.

She was extremely supportive of other creative people and held 'salons' in her home, a friendly and interesting way to bring like-minded people together.

Sarah's gravestone reads 'Fortis et Strenua', Latin for strong and active. She certainly was!

'We cannot live by bread alone, and it is a poor heart that never rejoices [in art].'

Sarah Purser

'I don't like this exclusion of women from the national fight.'

Maud Gonne

Maud Gonne

NATIONALIST AND ACTIVIST

1866–1953

Maud was born in England but moved to Kildare as a teenager with her father. He was a British Army officer who sadly died when she was twenty, leaving her an orphan. She hated injustice and as a young woman she protested against evictions of Irish families from their homes in Donegal. She used her inheritance to support this and many other causes.

In 1900 Queen Victoria visited Ireland, promising to treat 15,000 Irish children to sweet buns. But not everyone in Ireland was happy about the British monarch's reign over their country. So, to protest against this visit, Maud, along with other nationalist women, set up a 'Patriotic Treat' committee that beat the queen's goal by giving treats to 30,000 children: 20 tonnes of sweets, 40,000 buns and 1,000 oranges!

After this success, the women set up Inghinidhe na hÉireann (Daughters of Ireland), a society for Irish nationalist women. They held Irish-language and drama classes and promoted Irish products. Maud also published the first Irish newspaper for women, *Bean na hÉireann.*

Children were at the heart of many of Maud's campaigns and she set up a school dinner scheme to feed Dublin children, a service that is still offered to some children today.

During the Irish Civil War, Maud co-founded the Women's Prisoners Defence League to help all republican prisoners and their families. But the league was banned and Maud was imprisoned. Again, she protested, this time by going on hunger strike.

Maud is buried in the republican plot in Glasnevin Cemetery. She will always be remembered as a brave and passionate woman who showed other women how to use their voices.

Maud owned parrots, cats and canaries, a Great Dane dog called Dagda, and a marmoset monkey called Chaperone. She once had leather boots made to protect Dagda's paws.

She was almost six feet tall and was known as a great beauty and a force of nature. She inspired W.B. Yeats to write some of his greatest poetry. He asked her to marry him many times, but Maud always refused.

Maud's son, Seán MacBride, became a respected Irish politician. He won the Nobel Peace Prize in 1974 and was one of the founders of Amnesty International.

Anne Sullivan

GROUNDBREAKING TEACHER

1866–1936

Johanna 'Anne' Mansfield Sullivan's parents were from Limerick but left during the Irish Famine. When Anne was eight, her mum died and she was sent to a poorhouse in Tewksbury, Massachusetts.

She caught an eye infection that left her practically blind, but she was a clever, determined girl who desperately wanted an education. She begged to attend the Perkins School for the Blind in Boston and, aged twenty, graduated as one of their top students.

So when Helen Keller's parents wrote looking for a teacher for their deaf-blind daughter, the school recommended Anne. From the moment she met Helen, Anne began to sign words onto the six-year-old's hand, helping her understand that everything has a name. Anne also used touch, taste and smell in her lessons. It was hard work, but Anne knew her pupil had huge potential and she never gave up.

She encouraged Helen to put her hand on Anne's mouth and throat while she spoke, so she could recognise the vibrations. Eventually Helen was able to mimic these with her own mouth. The first word she spoke was 'it'.

Helen became famous and travelled all over the world with Anne, giving speeches. Together they changed the way people with special needs were viewed, as world citizens with something important to say.

Friends for over fifty years, Helen was holding Anne's hand when her beloved teacher died. Their ashes are buried together at the National Cathedral in Washington, D.C.

Helen said: 'Anne was a trail-blazer, day by day, month after month, year in and year out, she laboured to provide me with a voice.'

In 1930 Anne visited Ireland with Helen. Anne found the trip sad as it reminded her of how her parents were forced to leave 'the land of their birth'.

There are many photos and video clips of Anne and Helen together, and in most of them they are holding hands.

'Children require guidance and sympathy far more than instruction.'

Anne Sullivan

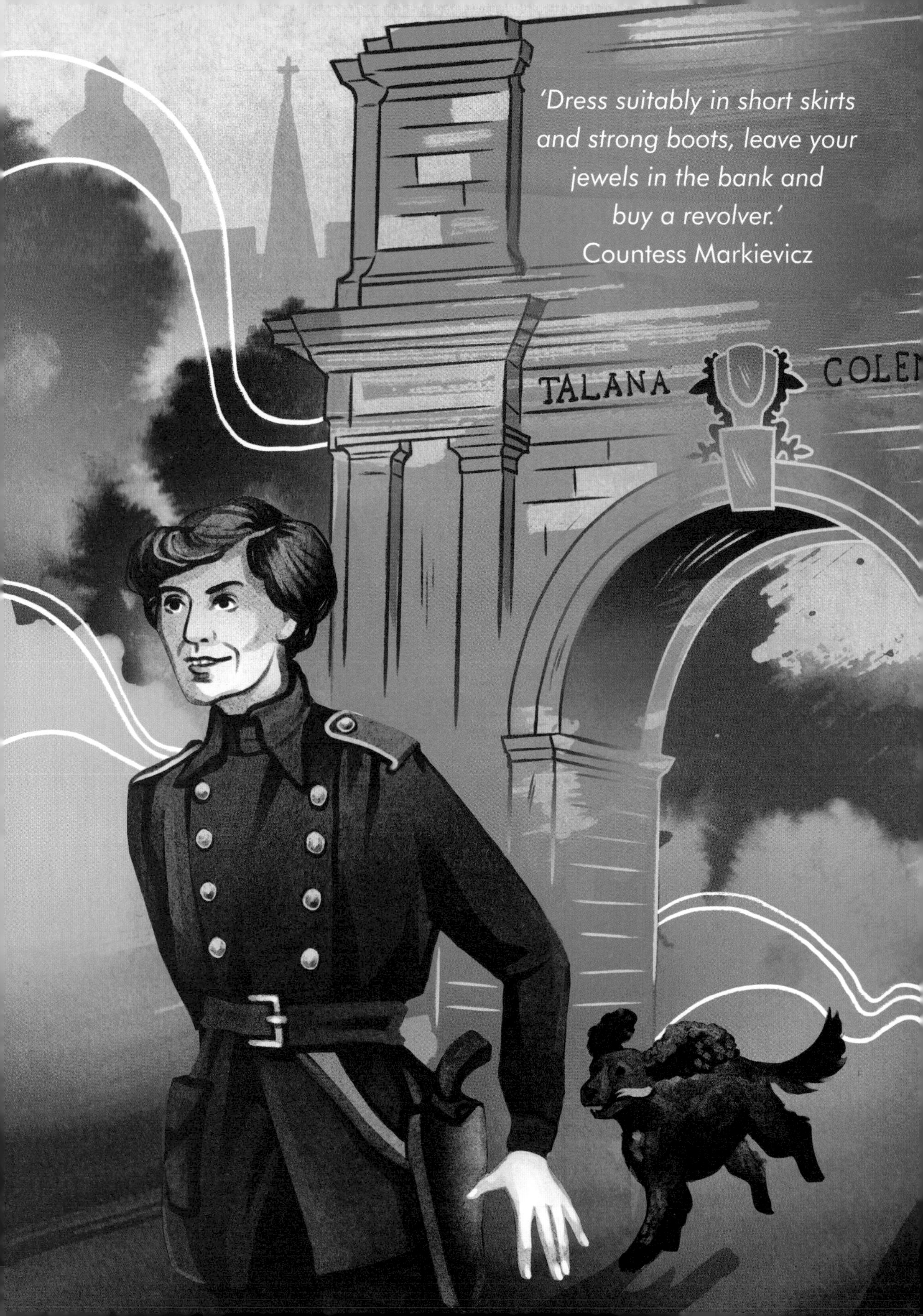

'Dress suitably in short skirts and strong boots, leave your jewels in the bank and buy a revolver.'
Countess Markievicz
TALANA
COLEN

Countess Markievicz

REBEL LEADER AND POLITICIAN

1868–1927

Constance Georgine Gore-Booth grew up in Lissadell House in Sligo, a grand house with large gardens. She was a gifted horsewoman and loved to ride and shoot.

She studied art in London and Paris. When she married Count Casimir Dunin-Markievicz, a dashing Polish aristocrat, Constance became Countess Markievicz.

In 1908 at the age of forty, looking for 'something to live for, something to die for', Constance joined Inghinidhe na hÉireann (Daughters of Ireland). She arrived at her first meeting in a satin ball gown and diamond tiara! There she met Maud Gonne and other revolutionary women and began to realise that 'there can be no free women in an enslaved nation'.

During the 1916 Easter Rising, Constance was second in command of the regiment at St Stephen's Green. Afterwards, the British government sentenced her to death but she was spared for being a woman and imprisoned instead. She was released in 1917 and in the 1918 general election she became the first woman to be elected to the British House of Commons. However, like her fellow Sinn Féin members, she refused to take her seat.

Instead, she was made Minister for Labour in Ireland's first Dáil, making her the first female cabinet minister in Ireland – and only the second in the world. But she spent much of this time in prison and in total spent more than three years behind bars.

Constance often suffered ill health and she sadly died aged only fifty-nine. She left all her money to the poor of Ireland. At her funeral, thousands of people came to pay their respects to this brave, unconventional and inspiring Irish woman.

Constance was a co-founder of Na Fianna Éireann, 'boy scouts for revolutionaries'. She took the boys camping and taught them how to march and use real firearms, so that one day they could fight for Ireland's freedom.

She was very close to her sister, Eva, who was a poet and campaigner for women's suffrage. Eva wrote many poems for and about her much-loved sister.

Constance loved dogs. There is a statue of her with Poppet, her favourite cocker spaniel, on Dublin's Townsend Street.

Aleen Cust

IRELAND'S FIRST FEMALE VET

1868–1937

As a child, Aleen loved to ride horses and play with dogs at her house in Tipperary. She and her brothers were educated together at home. But, when their father died, they moved to Shropshire in England.

When she grew up, Aleen started training as a nurse but switched to veterinary medicine in Edinburgh. Her family were not happy about this, and she had to pay her own college fees.

It wasn't easy coming first in her class, but Aleen studied hard and ignored the jeers of her fellow male students. Alas, Aleen was not allowed to sit her final professional veterinary exams because she was a woman. Instead, she found work as an assistant to William Byrne, a vet in County Roscommon.

In 1905 Aleen was made part-time Veterinary Inspector for County Galway, a remarkable achievement for a woman in the early twentieth century. Her new job caused a public outrage. 'We can understand women educating themselves to tend women – but horses! Good heavens!' said *The Ballinasloe News*.

When William Byrne died, Aleen took over his practice. She only made the wealthy pay, often gave money to the poor, and supplied free goat's milk to St Ultan's Children's Hospital in Dublin. She was a tall, strong, elegant woman with a warm heart. In 1922, twenty-seven years after graduation, Aleen was finally allowed to sit her professional veterinary exams and she became the first qualified woman vet in Ireland and Britain. Aleen died on a trip to Jamaica, just after treating a friend's dog, an animal lover to the very end.

Aleen kept curls of hair from her favourite horses and dogs in a locket she wore around her neck.

During the First World War, she looked after sick and injured war horses in France. Later, back in Ireland, she rode to her vet visits on a white Arabian stallion.

Aleen raised all kinds of animals at her home: cats, cocker spaniels, Jersey cows, Kerry cows, Pomeranians, quail and even ornamental pheasants!

'I have had the inestimable
privilege of attaining my life's
ambition … due to many
things: Fate, Luck, Tenacity.'
Aleen Cust

'The child is the nation's most precious possession.'

Dr Kathleen Lynn

Dr Kathleen Lynn

DOCTOR AND NATIONALIST

1874–1955

Not many doctors have shots fired over their coffins, but Kathleen Lynn was no ordinary doctor!

Kathleen was born in County Mayo and she grew up with illness and poverty all around her. Her father was a clergyman, and Kathleen and her mother made regular visits to the poor families in their parish, bringing food and nursing sick children.

She was taught at home before attending Alexandra College in Dublin. Her grandfather and cousin were doctors and she decided to become one too, which was very unusual for women at the time. She was a brilliant student and in her medical exams she won a medal for coming first in practical anatomy. After graduating, she opened her own doctor's surgery in Rathmines.

Kathleen was also a suffragette and a devoted nationalist. During the 1916 Easter Rising, she treated the wounded at City Hall. She was captured and imprisoned in Kilmainham Gaol. After she was freed, the authorities spied on her home for many years.

In 1919, thousands of Dublin children were dying before their first birthday. To combat this, Kathleen and her lifelong partner, Madeleine ffrench Mullen, opened St Ultan's Hospital, which was the very first children's hospital in Ireland. All of the staff in Kathleen's hospital were women.

Kathleen worked in the hospital almost until her death at the age of eighty-one. On the day of her funeral, as her coffin passed by, all of the nurses at St Ultan's stood on the nearby streets in their uniforms. They were showing their respect for this remarkable woman and saying their final goodbye.

Kathleen was a small woman who wore her hair in plaits, rode her bicycle everywhere and was fluent in German. Small in size, but big in brains and bravery!

She had a special balcony outside her bedroom so that she could sleep in the healthy fresh air, even in the middle of winter!

Kathleen said: 'Babies must be loved if they [are] to be cured.' She often gave long hugs to the babies and children in her hospital.

Hanna Sheehy Skeffington

SUFFRAGETTE, NATIONALIST AND HUMAN-RIGHTS CAMPAIGNER

1877–1946

Johanna 'Hanna' Mary Sheehy was born in Cork and moved to Dublin as a child. She grew up in a political family: her father was a nationalist MP, her mother believed in women's rights, and her uncle was a 'rebel priest'.

Hanna was an independent thinker from a young age and became one of the first women to graduate from an Irish university. She was a warm, hard-working and wise woman who believed strongly in equality for everyone. When she married Frank Skeffington, they took each other's names as a sign of their equality.

In 1908 Hanna and Frank helped set up the Irish Women's Franchise League (IWFL) and launched a feminist newspaper, *The Irish Citizen*. The Irish Parliamentary Party refused to support votes for women and many of the IWFL were outraged, including Hanna. In protest, they broke windows in Dublin Castle and were put in Mountjoy Prison for a month. Hanna went on hunger strike and was released after five days.

During the 1916 Easter Rising, Hanna and Frank helped the injured and brought food and messages to the rebels. Frank was captured and shot without trial. Devastated and angry, Hanna refused to take compensation money from the British Army and instead forced them to hold an inquiry into Frank's death. But Hanna didn't let her loss stop her, and for the next few years she travelled the world, speaking out about votes for women and Ireland's right to independence. She even spoke at Carnegie Hall in New York. She campaigned for the causes she so dearly believed in until her death. Hanna is buried in Glasnevin Cemetery with her husband.

Hanna and Frank's son, Owen Lancelot, became an Irish senator and, like his parents, became a champion for human rights.

She co-founded the Women's Prisoners Defence League and the Women's Social and Progressive League. Maud Gonne called her 'the ablest of all the fearless women who worked for Ireland's freedom'.

In 1937, Hanna and others objected to the definition of the role of women in the new Irish Constitution. It was less equal than they had fought for in the 1916 Rising.

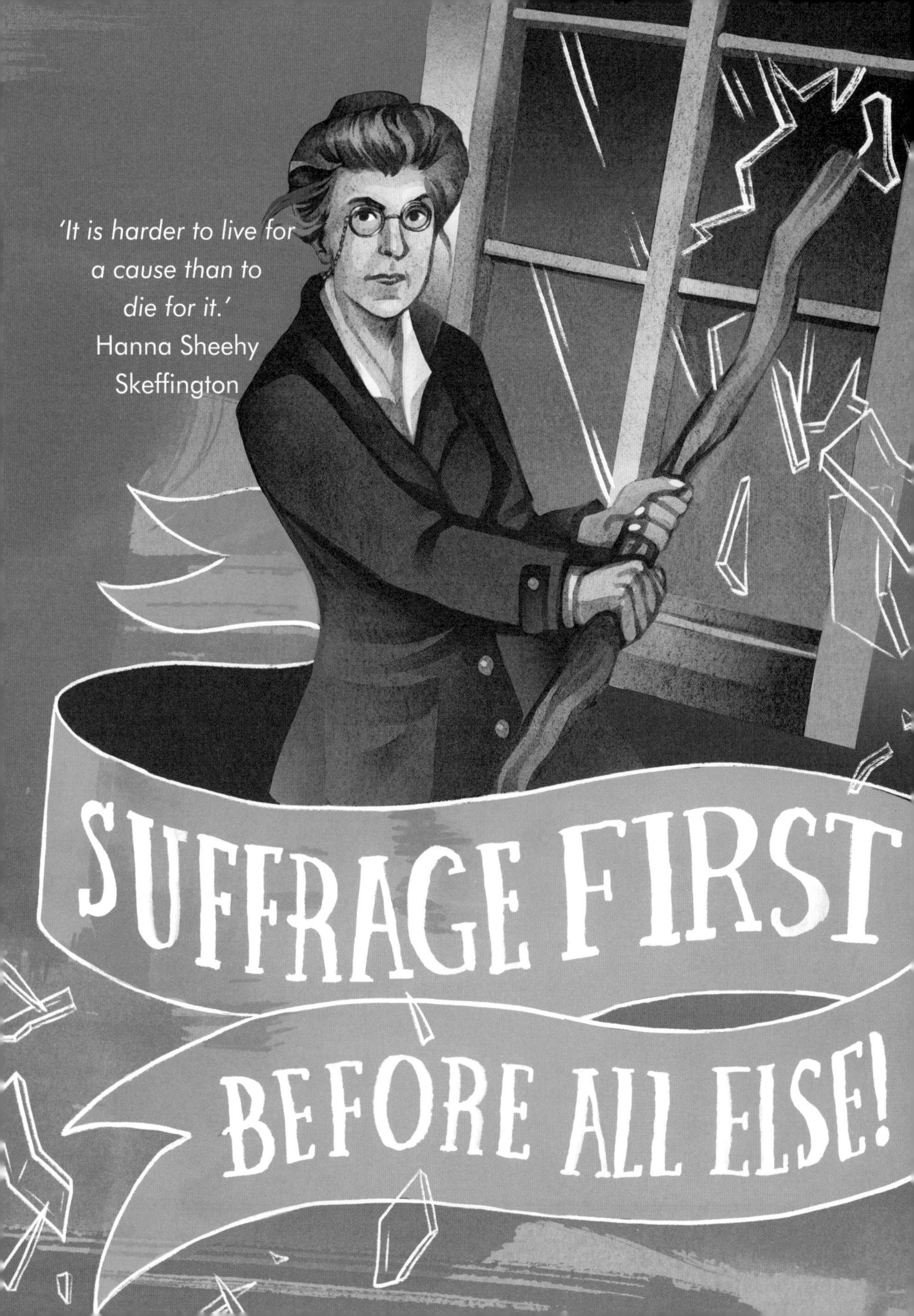

'It is harder to live for a cause than to die for it.'
Hanna Sheehy Skeffington

SUFFRAGE FIRST BEFORE ALL ELSE!

'My only difficulty is to prevent Mayfly flying when I do not want her to.'

Lillian Bland

Lilian Bland

PIONEERING AVIATOR

1878–1971

Even though Lilian Emily Bland was fascinated by birds from an early age, she never dreamed she would actually fly one day. But she became the first woman in the world to design, build and fly her own biplane.

As a girl Lilian loved riding horses and was brilliant at shooting. When she grew up, she became an award-winning photographer. She took some of the first colour pictures of live birds in the world. She was also one of the very first women sports journalists and wrote for London newspapers.

In 1909 Lilian was sent a postcard with the measurements of a famous monoplane that had crossed the English Channel. She decided to build a scale model of the biplane glider and make it fly near her family's home in County Antrim. She built it from bamboo, ash and elm and called it *Mayfly*. 'May fly, may not fly,' she joked.

She bought a twenty-horsepower, two-stroke engine and made her own fuel system from a whiskey bottle and her aunt's ear trumpet! *Mayfly* rose thirty feet off the ground and was the first ever Irish biplane to fly.

In 1911 she married her cousin, Charles Loftus Bland from Vancouver Island, Canada. After their young daughter died, Lilian retired to Cornwall where she painted, gambled and gardened until her death in 1971.

Annie 'Nancy' Corrigan was from Achill Island but she learned to fly in America and trained fighter pilots during the Second World War. She became only the second female commercial pilot in America, flying over 600,000 miles during her career.

Dame Mary Bailey, from Rossmore Castle, County Monaghan, was awarded her pilot's licence in 1927, and was the first woman to fly across the Irish Sea. She was known as one of the finest pilots of her time.

In 1977, Gráinne Cronin became the first female commercial pilot to fly for an Irish airline, Aer Lingus. She was made a captain in 1988 and retired in 2010.

Eileen Gray

DESIGNER AND ARCHITECT

1878–1976

Kathleen Eileen Moray Smith, better known as Eileen Gray, grew up in a big house in Enniscorthy, County Wexford. Keen to be independent and creative, she enrolled in art school in London when she was twenty.

On a visit to the Victoria and Albert Museum, Eileen fell in love with Japanese lacquer, a hard, glossy substance made from tree resin. She became an expert in using it to decorate screens and furniture.

In 1900 she moved to Paris to begin working as an interior architect. She created startling, extravagant rooms for rich Parisians. Some of her designs were so original and ahead of their time they baffled critics – Eileen Gray was that good! She designed furniture and rugs and sold them from her shop, where the writer James Joyce was a customer.

Then, in 1926, she started designing a house in France which she called E-1027 (the 'E' stands for Eileen). She wanted it to be both practical and comfortable. 'A house is not a machine to live in,' she said. People from all over the world still visit E-1027 to wonder at its clever design.

Eileen continued to work well into her nineties. Her ashes are buried in Père Lachaise cemetery in Paris. Forgotten for many years, her furniture is now considered classic and is still made today. She is celebrated as one of the world's most influential designers.

Eileen loved cars and flying. Her first car was a Chenard-Walcker in 1909. She flew from Mexico City to Acapulco in an airmail plane in the 1930s, a daring trip.

She is known as a pioneer of Modernism. E-1027 was the first Modernist building designed by a female architect. There is a small model of the house in the Irish Architectural Archive, Dublin.

Eileen's work is on show at the Victoria and Albert Museum, London, the Museum of Modern Art, New York, and the National Museum of Ireland at Collins Barracks in Dublin.

'To create one must first question everything.'
Eileen Gray

'What about us?
We want a game of our own!'
Máire Ní Chinnéide

Máire Ní Chinnéide

FOUNDER OF CAMOGIE AND IRISH-LANGUAGE ACTIVIST

1879–1967

Máire was born in Rathmines and went to Muckross Park College and then the Royal University, where she won the first Irish-language scholarship. With this, she became an Irish teacher and would later become the first woman president of Oireachtas na Gaeilge (the festival of Irish culture).

In 1903, Máire led the group that created camogie (originally 'camóguidheacht'). Around this time many Irish people were rediscovering their language, culture and sports. Máire and her camogie teammates were right on trend! She became the first president of the Camogie Association. And she scored the very first goal in competitive camogie on 17 July 1904. Over a century later, one of the inter-county All Ireland Championship trophies is named in Máire's honour.

In 1932 Máire visited the Blasket Islands, off the coast of Kerry, with her daughter, Niamh, and met a remarkable woman called Peig Sayers, who told her sad but unique stories about how hard it was to live on the islands. Máire believed everyone should hear about Peig's life, so Peig dictated her stories to her son, Mícheál, and Máire edited them before they were published.

Máire was also an accomplished author herself: she wrote children's plays and translated *Grimms' Fairy Tales* into Irish. She loved the Irish language and spent her life promoting it and Irish culture.

For over one hundred years, girls and women all over Ireland and the world have enjoyed playing camogie thanks to Máire's determination to include women in Ireland's Gaelic revival.

Máire's work blazed a trail for extraordinary camogie players like Angela Downey and her twin sister, Ann Downey (twelve All Ireland medals each), and Kay Mills (fifteen All Ireland medals). Beat that!

Students all over Ireland read *Peig* for their Leaving Certificate Irish exam. Not everyone liked it – it's very sad and the Irish is quite tricky. But everyone remembers it!

In the early days, girls were so nervous about carrying their hurleys in public that they wrapped them in brown paper.

Lady Heath

AVIATOR AND OLYMPIAN

1896–1939

Sophie Mary Pierce-Evans was born in Limerick. She was brought up by her grandfather and aunts, who called her simply 'Mary'. Later, she became Lady Heath when she married Sir James Heath, an English politician, in 1927.

Mary had a brave and adventurous spirit. During the First World War she drove ambulances on the front line in France. In 1925 Mary took her first aeroplane ride. She was hooked!

At the time women were not allowed to be commercial pilots, but Mary was keen to show everyone exactly what female pilots could do. She was the first woman in the world to fly a loop the loop and the first to parachute jump from an aeroplane.

But what made her world-famous was her solo flight from Cape Town in South Africa to London in early 1928, taking a gruelling 16,000 kilometre route. Newspapers all over the globe wrote about her record-breaking journey.

As well as being a famous aviator, Mary was also an accomplished athlete. She was six feet tall and very strong. She set new world records in both the high jump and the javelin. But in the early twentieth century, sport was called 'unladylike' and 'bad' for girls. Women were not allowed to compete in the Olympics. Mary thought this was nonsense and fought to change it. So, it was thanks to Mary's hard work that women were allowed to compete in athletics and gymnastics in 1928.

Mary died in 1939 and it is said her ashes were scattered from an aeroplane over Newcastle West in County Limerick. A fitting end for one of Ireland's most daring women!

Mary helped set up the Junior Aviation Club in Ireland, the first flying club for teenagers in Europe.

Her plane – an Avro Avian monoplane painted silver and blue – was later owned by Amelia Earhart. A small model of it is on display at The Little Museum of Dublin.

Mary's flying kit for her Cape Town–London flight included books, a tennis racket, evening dresses and a fur coat! Even after her epic trip she looked like a movie star.

'To fly is an adventure.'

Lady Heath

Mainie Jellett

ARTIST AND DESIGNER

1897–1944

Mary Harriet 'Mainie' Jellett grew up in Dublin City. She loved drawing from an early age and studied at the Metropolitan School of Art in Dublin, before moving to the Westminster School of Art, London. She then studied with Cubist painters André Lhote and Albert Gleizes in Paris. In London she met a lifelong friend, the Irish artist Evie Hone.

Mainie's paintings were abstract* and she brought together old religious ideas and Celtic design with new styles of painting. In 1923 she showed work, including a piece called 'Decoration', in the Dublin Painters' Exhibition but her paintings were laughed at. The newspapers called them 'freak pictures' and 'an insoluble puzzle' because they looked so different to traditional paintings. They were full of geometric shapes and vivid colours, and some even called them 'foreign' and 'dangerous'!

But that didn't stop Mainie as she was determined to bring Modernism to Irish people. She gave lectures about modern art and taught art to children and adults. She co-founded the Irish Exhibition of Living Art in 1943, the first modern art exhibition in Ireland.

In time people began to accept and even like Mainie's art, and she is now seen as one of Ireland's first Modernist artists. 'Decoration' is in the National Gallery of Ireland's collection and is considered one of the most important Irish abstract paintings.

**Abstract art is made up of colours, lines and shapes put together in an expressive way. Cubism is a type of abstract art.*

One of Mainie's first art teachers was Lolly Yeats, whose brother was the poet W.B. Yeats. Lolly also ran a publishing house called Cuala Press.

Mainie also designed costumes and sets for the theatre, and textiles and rugs. She had a practical view of design: houses should reflect their owners' personalities and not be designed simply to impress, she said.

Evie Hone became a highly respected stained glass artist, making over fifty windows including the east window at Eton College Chapel in Windsor, England.

'Look at these pictures with an open mind.'
Mainie Jellett

'You cannot create genius.
All you can do is nurture it.'
Dame Ninette de Valois

Dame Ninette de Valois

FOUNDER OF THE ROYAL BALLET

1898–2001

Edris Stannus, who later took the glamorous stage name Ninette de Valois, loved to dance and dreamed of being a ballerina. After her family moved from Wicklow to London in 1905, she attended a stage school and performed in many pantomimes and plays.

When she was older, she paid for ballet lessons herself by working in a hospital kitchen and teaching children to dance. In 1923 her hard work paid off: Ninette joined the world-famous Ballets Russes and toured with the Russian company.

But when she discovered she had polio, a disease of the muscles, she knew she'd have to stop dancing. She decided to do something incredible instead – she opened a ballet school and then set up the first British ballet company. It was a bold move, but Ninette was as brave and determined as they come.

She made a deal with the Sadler's Wells Theatre in London and used the money from her ballet school to pay dancers and produce shows. During the Second World War she took her company on tour and gave audiences some much-needed entertainment. After the war, her company moved to the Royal Opera House in Covent Garden and changed its name to the Royal Ballet.

Margot Fonteyn, one of the most famous ballerinas of all time, was discovered and trained by Ninette. As well as being a gifted teacher, Ninette was also a highly respected choreographer, creating over forty new ballets including *Checkmate*. She spent her 100th birthday watching her Royal Ballet School students dance. 'Classical ballet will never die,' she said. And wasn't she right?

Ninette was such a shy girl that when she arrived at other children's parties she'd be sick, cry and beg to be taken home.

In 1926 Ninette produced and performed in *Four Plays for Dancers* in the Abbey Theatre in Dublin, which was written by W.B. Yeats.

Joan Denise Moriarty set up the Irish National Ballet, the first professional ballet company in Ireland. Ninette was one of its patrons.

Dame Kathleen Lonsdale

CRYSTALLOGRAPHER

1903–1971

Not many people have a diamond named after them – the Lonsdaleite – but Kathleen Lonsdale was a rather remarkable scientist!

Born Kathleen Yardley in Newbridge, County Kildare, the youngest of ten children, she moved to England when she was a child. Her school did not teach science to girls so she studied it at the local boys' school. Kathleen won a county scholarship and started college at only sixteen. She got top marks in all her physics exams.

In 1922, the Nobel Prize-winning physicist Professor William Bragg invited Kathleen to join the research school at University College London to work in the brand-new area of X-ray crystallography (the study of the structure of crystals). Kathleen was brilliant at her work and she adored it. 'It was exciting to find new facts,' she said.

Kathleen made a ground-breaking discovery when she proved that the shape of the benzene ring is flat. This was something chemists had argued about for decades. Benzene is used to make plastics. She also did important work on diamonds and how they are formed.

Kathleen was a pacifist and refused to sign up for duty during the Second World War. For this she was sent to Holloway Prison for one month. This began her lifelong interest in making prisons better. She was a leader in the world of crystallography and, in 1949, she became the first woman professor in University College London. She spent the rest of her life teaching and travelling the world, talking about the glory of crystals and encouraging girls to study science.

Kathleen's life was full of remarkable firsts: in 1945 she was one of the first two women to become fellows of the Royal Society, the oldest national scientific society in the world.

When she was made a dame by Queen Elizabeth II at Buckingham Palace, Kathleen made her own hat using lace, coloured card and ribbons.

Kathleen believed that for a married woman with children to become a first-class scientist, she must first choose the right husband. Her own husband, Thomas Jackson Lonsdale, fully supported her career and even cut her hair for her!

'My work was fun. I often ran the last few yards to the laboratory.'

Dame Kathleen Lonsdale

'I have acted, punched, swash-buckled, and shot my way through an absurdly masculine profession … I made my mark on my own terms.'

Maureen O'Hara

Maureen O'Hara

ACTOR AND BUSINESSWOMAN

1920–2015

Maureen FitzSimons grew up in Ranelagh in Dublin and was a naturally gifted performer from a young age. She joined the Abbey Theatre when she was fourteen and signed her first Hollywood film contract at only seventeen.

With the stage name Maureen O'Hara, she starred in over fifty films, including *Miracle on 34th Street* and *The Parent Trap*. She worked with some of the greatest male directors of the time, from Alfred Hitchcock to John Ford, and her leading men included Tyrone Power and Errol Flynn. Her favourite and most famous role was as fiery Irishwoman Mary Kate Danaher in *The Quiet Man*, opposite John Wayne's Irish-American boxer. Maureen and 'Duke', as she liked to call Wayne, starred in four more films together and became lifelong friends.

Maureen was strong and sporty. She loved action roles and insisted on performing most of her own stunts. 'The film studio thought I was crazy,' she said, 'but I loved it.' In 1945 she was the first to stand up to sexism in Hollywood, saying, 'I don't let the producer and director kiss me'. She fought for better pay and equal billing on film posters. The studio heads and directors didn't always like her, but they definitely respected her.

In 1968 she married a pilot called Charles Blair. When he died in a plane crash, she took over the running of their Caribbean seaplane company, becoming the first female president of a commercial airline.

Maureen's star on the Hollywood Walk of Fame was unveiled in February 1960. She will be remembered as Ireland's first Hollywood superstar.

Maureen's dad, Charles, was part-owner of Shamrock Rovers Football Club in Dublin, and she was a lifelong supporter of the team, saying when she was young all she wanted was to play for them.

Sara Allgood, from Drumcondra, starred with Maureen in *How Green Was My Valley*. Greer Garson, whose parents were from County Down, won an Oscar in 1943 for her leading role in *Mrs Miniver*.

Maureen always told younger female actors: 'Never give up. Stick to it, and hustle.' She published her autobiography, *'Tis Herself*, in 2004.

Sybil Connolly

FASHION DESIGNER AND BUSINESSWOMAN

1921–1998

Sybil Connolly was born in Wales. Her father was Irish and her mother was Welsh. As a girl she loved fashion and design. She lived in Waterford as a teenager before travelling to London aged seventeen to study dressmaking.

In 1940 she moved to Dublin to work as a manager in the Richard Alan shop and later became their designer. She was a stylish, hard-working woman who was full of energy.

Sybil launched her own fashion label in Dublin at the age of thirty-six; she was the first woman to run an Irish-based fashion house. She employed around one hundred Irish women, who made lace and knitwear for her designs. She liked to use traditional Irish fabrics like tweed but was best known for the way she used finely pleated linen called 'handkerchief' linen.

Carmel Snow, the dynamic Irish-born editor of New York fashion magazine *Harper's Bazaar* brought Sybil's work to America by inviting a group of American journalists to a fashion show featuring Sybil's designs at Dunsany Castle in County Meath. The journalists were very impressed with Sybil, calling her 'a milk-skinned Irish charmer', and wrote about her clothes in their newspapers and magazines.

The actors Julie Andrews and Elizabeth Taylor wore Sybil's elegant dresses, but her most famous client was Jacqueline Kennedy, former First Lady of America.

Ireland in the early 1950s wasn't known for its style or fashion. But Sybil changed all that and will always be remembered as the woman who first put Ireland on the international fashion map.

Sybil once made a summer dress from striped linen tea towels. She called it 'Kitchen Fugue'.

In 1953 *Life* magazine featured one of Sybil's dramatic red cloaks on their cover with the headline 'Irish Invade Fashion World'.

Sybil's designs are still loved. Actor Gillian Anderson (star of 'The X-Files') wore a vintage 1950s Sybil Connolly evening gown to the BAFTA Awards in 2012.

'[A]s long as we can show such beauty in design ... we cannot ever be called a vanishing race.'
Sybil Connolly

'I just knew I loved math; that was the only thing I was really good at.'

Kay McNulty Mauchly Antonelli

Kay McNulty Mauchly Antonelli

DIGITAL COMPUTER PROGRAMMER

1921–2006

Kathleen Rita 'Kay' McNulty was born in Donegal to an Irish-speaking family who emigrated to Philadelphia. She adored maths and studied algebra and geometry in high school. In college she took every maths course she could find.

After graduating, Kay was hired by the US Army's Ballistic Research Lab as a 'human computer'. During the Second World War, her job was to work out ballistics trajectories: how far guns and canons would shoot bullets and missiles. Kay and her female colleagues did this by hand using graph paper and mechanical desk calculators, and it could take nearly two days to figure out one sum!

ENIAC (Electronic Numerical Integrator and Computer) was one of the world's first electronic digital computers, and Kay was chosen to be one of its first six programmers. It took the computer ten seconds to do one sum, but it could take two or three days to set the machine's plugs and switches to solve a new problem – this was Kay's job. There was no manual for ENIAC; the programmers had to figure out how the machine worked using the blueprints and programme it by hand.

Kay never gave up her passion for computers, working as a software designer, writing articles and giving talks about computing and the ENIAC project for the rest of her life.

ENIAC was huge – it was made up of forty black modules that were eight feet high, 18,000 vacuum tubes and 3,000 switches – and it filled a large room. But its total processing power can now fit on a chip about the size of a ten-cent coin.

At the press launch for ENIAC, the programmers were asked only to act as 'hostesses'. Kay said they felt like models demonstrating a new fridge, not maths whizzes!

In 1997 Kay was inducted into the Women in Technology International Hall of Fame with her five ENIAC programming sisters.

Maeve Kyle

IRELAND'S FIRST FEMALE OLYMPIAN

1928

As a girl, Maeve Shankey could run like the wind. She grew up in Kilkenny and later went to Alexandra College, Dublin. She was a gifted hockey player and she played for the Leinster senior team as a teenager. She went on to play for Ireland fifty-eight times. In 1953 she met Seán Kyle, who became both her running coach and her husband. The following year they set up Ballymena and Antrim Athletics Club, and Maeve was one of their star athletes.

Maeve was selected to run at the 1956 Olympics in Melbourne, Australia. She was the first woman to compete for Ireland at the Games, but instead of being proud, people were outraged! They said it was 'unladylike', and letters of complaint were sent to the newspapers. Maeve was shouted at in the streets of Ireland, and things were thrown at her while she was out training. But Maeve refused to let it stop her. She said: 'I grew up with a belief I was perfectly entitled to do what the boys were doing.' That year, she represented Ireland in the 100m and the 200m races, and she ran again in the 1960 Olympics in Rome and the 1964 Olympics in Tokyo.

Maeve went on to win over thirty medals in international championships and set new world records. She also became a coach so that she 'could help other young athletes to … achieve the Olympic dream'. Her skill and determination paved the way for future Irish women athletes like Gina Akpe-Moses, Catherina McKiernan, Derval O'Rourke and Sonia O'Sullivan.

Maeve raised some of the money to travel to Melbourne herself – £200, a huge sum at the time.

The first Irish-born woman to win an Olympic medal was an archer Beatrice Geraldine Hill-Lowe, who won a bronze in the 1908 Olympics in London.

Lena Rice, from County Tipperary, won Wimbledon in 1890 and is said to have invented the forehand smash.

'Somebody had to be first.'

Maeve Kyle

'We are all made of star stuff.'

Dame Jocelyn Bell Burnell

Dame Jocelyn Bell Burnell

ASTROPHYSICIST

1943

Growing up near Belfast, Jocelyn loved space. She wanted to study science at school but girls were only allowed to take home economics instead! Her parents were able to change the teachers' minds, and Jocelyn went on to study physics at the University of Glasgow, the only woman in her year.

When she was attending her lectures, the boys would wolf whistle at her, but she ignored them and graduated in 1965 with honours. While studying for her doctorate at the University of Cambridge she helped build a huge radio telescope. It was her job to interpret the printouts of radio transmissions coming from space, up to one hundred feet per day, the length of almost two double-decker buses!

Studying the readouts, she discovered radio waves pulsing from deep space. Jocelyn proved that these waves came from small, dense stars. She had discovered pulsars – a new kind of star! Pulsars behave in strange and unusual ways, and they enable scientists to learn more about the universe and how it works. Jocelyn's discovery helped her male supervisors win a Nobel Prize for Physics in 1974. Many scientists still feel that Jocelyn should have shared in the award, but she says: 'I've had so many other awards, it's been amazing ... The world's not fair and it's how you cope with the world's unfairness that counts.'

Jocelyn was the first female president of the Institute of Physics. 'For me, being a role model [is] important,' she says. 'Just to show there are women doing science, enjoying it and being good at it.' To this day Jocelyn continues to study space.

Jocelyn failed her 11+ exam, but she didn't let it stop her. In secondary school in York she found a good teacher who showed her 'how easy physics was', and she never looked back.

Her dad was an architect who worked on the Armagh Planetarium. 'I became interested in astronomy through reading my dad's books,' she said.

The pulsar signals were nicknamed 'LGM' or Little Green Men, as some people thought the signals were made by aliens. Jocelyn knew better!

Anne O'Brien

PROFESSIONAL INTERNATIONAL FOOTBALLER

1956–2016

As a young girl, Anne loved playing football around the streets of Inchicore in Dublin. 'I always had a ball on my foot,' she said. Football was in her blood: she was related to footballers Johnny Giles and Jimmy Conway.

In her teens, Anne joined a women's factory football team, Vards. Then she played for the Dublin All-Stars team. And then, in 1973, a French coach spotted Anne on the pitch and asked her to join his women's football team, Stade de Reims.

Even though Anne was only seventeen and would be moving to France alone, she was determined to go and managed to convince her mum to let her travel. She was the first woman from Ireland or Britain to be signed to a professional European team. She was even featured on the BBC news. Within nine months of arriving, she was speaking fluent French.

Anne became known as an elegant and intelligent midfielder with brilliant timing and balance. When she moved to Lazio in Rome to play in the Italian Serie A, she learned yet another language. The Italian players were tough, but Anne had grown up playing football on the streets of Dublin and was every bit as strong.

During her hugely successful eighteen-year career, Anne won eleven league titles in Italy. She also won the league and cup in France with Stade de Reims. On retiring, she qualified as a football coach, working with youth teams and passing on her love of the sport.

After her death, the Football Association of Ireland said Anne would 'be remembered as one of the country's greatest ever female footballers'.

Anne never wanted a doll for Christmas; she wanted an Annie Oakley toy set or a ball.

She wore the number 10 jersey for the Lazio team. Italian women's football legend Carolina Morace called Anne 'an inspiration'.

A few weeks after her son Andrea was born, Anne went back to playing football and breastfed him before and after matches.

*'If you have talent,
you can go anywhere.'*
Anne O'Brien

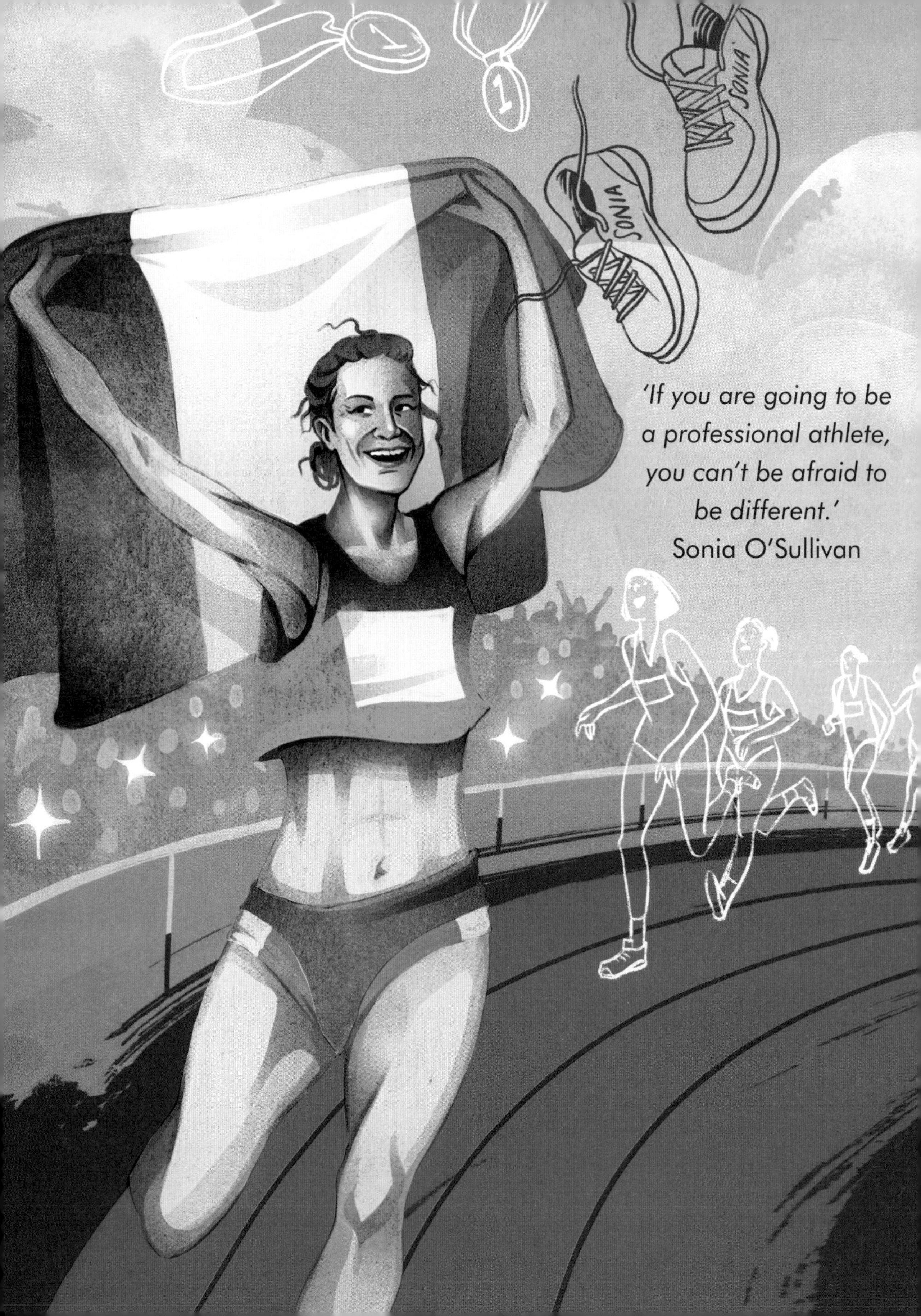

'If you are going to be a professional athlete, you can't be afraid to be different.'

Sonia O'Sullivan

Sonia O'Sullivan

WORLD CHAMPION ATHLETE

1969

Sonia is Ireland's most successful female athlete ever, and is much loved for her fighting spirit. She won three World Championships, three European Championships, broke four world records and ran for Ireland in four Olympic Games.

She originally joined the local athletics club Ballymore Cobh for the discos, but soon started winning races. At seventeen she won the National Junior Cross Country Championships and only a week later won the senior title. Ireland had never seen such a natural champion, and the world also began to take notice.

After secondary school Sonia accepted a life-changing athletics scholarship to Villanova University in Pennsylvania, USA. Her early years there were not easy but she was focussed and never gave up. She graduated in 1992 with a degree in accountancy. By then she was the college's star runner. That same year she represented Ireland in her first Olympics in Barcelona, setting six new Irish records and coming fourth in the 3,000 metres, an outstanding result for a young runner.

Over the next four years, Sonia became a European and world champion and a record-holder so that by the time of the Atlanta Olympic Games in 1996, she was the world's favourite. Sadly, though, she came away with no medals. But once again she picked herself up and kept running. Then, at the Sydney Olympics in 2000, she won a silver medal in the 5,000 metres race. Everyone in Ireland went wild and people were cheering in the streets!

Although Sonia retired in 2007, she still participates in charity runs and commentates about her beloved sport.

Sonia was famous for her 'finishing kick': she would hold back until the last 200 metres and then sprint past her competitors. She often did this final sprint in 27.5 seconds – incredibly fast!

Her 1994 world record for the outdoor 2,000 metres (5:25:36) has never been beaten.

Sonia's daughter Sophie is also a gifted athlete. She is an Australian and Irish champion in the 800 and 1,500 metres, and an Irish champion high jumper.

Mary Robinson

IRELAND'S FIRST FEMALE PRESIDENT

1944

Born Mary Therese Winifred Bourke in Ballina, County Mayo, the daughter of two doctors, Mary was a clever, determined student and worked hard at her studies. 'My parents let me know I had the same potential, the same opportunities, the same right to be whatever I wanted to be as my brothers,' she said.

After school she studied law at Trinity College, Dublin and won a fellowship to Harvard Law School in 1968. On campus, there were marches against the Vietnam War and debates about equality, race and gender. This made a lasting impression on Mary.

When she was only twenty-four, Mary became Reid Professor of Criminal Law in Trinity College and a year later was elected to the Seanad (Ireland's senate). For over twenty years she fought for human rights such as women's rights and Travellers' rights.

In 1990 she ran as an independent candidate for the Irish presidency. For the first time, many women voted for who they wanted as president and not who their husbands or fathers wanted. When Mary won the election, she thanked 'the women of Ireland, mná na hÉireann, who, instead of rocking the cradle, rocked the system'.

After her presidency she became United Nations High Commissioner for Human Rights and later set up the Mary Robinson Foundation – Climate Justice to help those most vulnerable to and least responsible for the effects of climate change. She is still fighting to give everyone in the world an equal say and is often considered a voice of reason and fairness during important international debates.

One of Mary's first media interviews as president was on 'The Den', a children's show on RTÉ. She talked to Ray D'Arcy, Zig and Zag and Dustin the Turkey!

Mary McAleese was Ireland's second female president. Her presidency was dedicated to 'building bridges' and promoting an Irish society where everyone is treated equally.

Mary Robinson is one of The Elders, a group of trusted world leaders. In 2009 Barack Obama awarded her the Presidential Medal of Freedom. He called her 'an advocate for the hungry and the hunted, the forgotten and the ignored'.

'I want women who
have felt themselves
outside history
to be written back
into history.'
Mary Robinson

BLAZING A TRAIL INTO THE FUTURE

These young Irishwomen are already making their mark on the twenty-first century. Now it's over to you. How will you make your mark? Will you be a scientist? An athlete? President of Ireland? It's time to blaze your trail!

Saoirse Ronan

ACTOR

Saoirse first appeared in Irish television's 'The Clinic', but her breakout role was in the film *Atonement*, for which she received her first Academy Award nomination, aged only thirteen. She won a 2018 Golden Globe Award for her role in *Lady Bird* and has become a true Hollywood A-lister.

Gina Akpe-Moses

ATHLETE

Gina was born in Lagos, Nigeria, and began running with St Gerald's Athletics Club in Dundalk when she was eight. She won a gold medal at the European Athletics Under-20 Championships in Italy in 2017. She loves running for Ireland and says hearing the national anthem played when she wins makes her very happy!

Annie and Kate Madden

SCIENTISTS AND BUSINESSWOMEN

Meath sisters Annie and Kate Madden grew up around horses. They won a BT Young Scientist Award at the ages of thirteen and fourteen for discovering natural solutions to soothe horses' tummies. Their company, FenuHealth, produces supplements for horses and racing camels, employs eight people and sells products into fifteen different countries.

Katie Taylor

OLYMPIC BOXER

Katie got her first pair of boxing gloves when she was ten. Just five years later, she made boxing history when she took part in the first official women's boxing match in Ireland. She went on to win countless world boxing titles and in 2012 won an Olympic gold medal for Ireland, one of the first ever for women's boxing.

Ruth Negga

ACTOR

Ruth was born in Addis Ababa, Ethiopia, and grew up in Limerick and studied acting at Trinity College, Dublin. For her outstanding portrayal of Mildred in *Loving*, she was nominated for a BAFTA, a Golden Globe and an Academy Award. She won an Irish Film and Television Award in 2012.

Sinéad Burke

ACADEMIC, ACTIVIST AND WRITER

Standing three feet, five inches tall, Dubliner Sinéad Burke dreams of a world where every person is encouraged and celebrated equally. She is helping make this a reality by speaking in schools, workplaces, even the White House, and to fashion designers about creating clothes for and with people with disabilities.

Louise O'Neill

WRITER AND ACTIVIST

Born in Cork, Louise's first Young Adult novel, *Only Ever Yours*, launched her onto the international literary stage like a rocket. She says when she's writing that's when she is her most honest. She is a committed feminist and talks to students around Ireland about women's rights.

About the Author

Sarah Webb is a writer for children and adults. *A Sailor Went to Sea, Sea, Sea: Favourite Rhymes from an Irish Childhood* (with Steve McCarthy), won the Irish Book Awards Children's Book of the Year (Junior) in 2017 and was shortlisted for the Children's Books Ireland Book of the Year Awards 2018. Sarah won the Children's Books Ireland Award for Outstanding Contribution to Children's Books in 2015.

Sarah also runs Story Crew: Write, Draw, Create, which provides writing clubs and creative workshops for children and the young at heart. She is the Children's Literary Advisor to Listowel Writers' Week.

Sarah has a great love of history and over the years has been inspired by many remarkable women, from her primary school English teacher Miss Cahill, to her history of art lecturer at Trinity College, Dubin, Professor Anne Crookshank.

www.sarahwebb.ie

About the Illustrator

Lauren O'Neill is a curly-haired, Wexford-born illustrator and graduate of NCAD who now lives and works in Dublin City. She lives with her husband, Dónal, and spends most of her time in or near her home studio, drawing, eating biscuits or going on nature walks with their dog, Smudge. She often does drawing workshops for children, usually learning more from them than they do from her.

Lauren's work can be found on the covers and insides of several books for children, and she is the proud winner of the Children's Books Ireland Honour Award for Illustration 2016 for *Gulliver*, Jonathan Swift's classic tale retold by Mary Webb, also published by The O'Brien Press.

www. laurenipsum.ie